Hans de Beer

Little Polar Bear

Kleiner Eisbär

wohin fährst du?

North-South Books · Nord-Süd Verlag

English translation by Rosemary Lanning
Lektorat Brigitte Hanhart Sidjanski

The text has been abridged for this dual language edition · Der Text wurde für die zweisprachige Ausgabe gekürzt.

© 2002 für die englisch/deutsche Ausgabe. © 1987 für die Originalausgabe Nord-Süd Verlag AG, Gossau Zürich und Hamburg
Alle Rechte, auch die der Bearbeitung oder auszugsweisen Vervielfältigung, gleich durch welche Medien, vorbehalten
Lithographie: Photolitho AG, Gossau Zürich · DTP/Satz: Pro Desk AG, Uster · Gesetzt in der Bauer Bodoni, 13 Punkt
Druck: Proost N.V., Turnhout
ISBN 3 314 01304 3
Die Deutsche Bibliothek – CIP-Einheitsaufnahme: Ein Titelsatz für diese Publikation ist bei der Deutschen Bibliothek erhältlich.

Besuchen Sie uns im Internet: www.nord-sued.com

Today was a special day for Lars, the little polar bear. His father was going to take him for his first trip across the ice fields to the sea. Lars lived with his parents at the North Pole, surrounded by ice and snow. This morning everything around him was as white as his fur. It was snowing.

Heute war ein besonderer Tag für Lars, den kleinen Eisbären. Zum ersten Mal durfte er mit seinem Vater aufs große Eis hinaus, bis zum Meer. Lars lebte mit seinen Eltern am Nordpol, mitten in Schnee und Eis. An diesem Morgen war die Welt um ihn herum so weiß wie sein Fell. Es schneite.

At about midday they reached the sea. Before them lay an endless expanse of blue. "Stay here and watch carefully how I swim," said Father Polar Bear, leaping into the cold water. He swam back and forth a few times, then suddenly dived under the water. Lars didn't see him again for a long time. He was getting quite worried, but then his father reappeared with a lovely big fish.

Gegen Mittag kamen sie zum Meer. Blau und endlos lag es vor ihnen. »Bleib hier und schau gut zu, wie ich schwimme!«, sagte Vater Eisbär und sprang ins kalte Wasser. Mehrmals schwamm er hin und her. Dann plötzlich tauchte er unter. Lars sah ihn lange nicht mehr. Es wurde ihm etwas bange. Doch da tauchte der Vater wieder auf, mit einem schönen, großen Fisch!

"Come on, this is our supper," said Father Polar Bear, biting the fish in half.
After they had eaten it was time to sleep. "Now, Lars, you must make a pile of snow,"
said Father Polar Bear, "to protect you from the cold wind." They pushed snow in front
of them until they had each made a heap. Lars was proud of his own windbreak, and
he snuggled down contentedly on the snow. Soon they were both asleep.

»Komm, das ist unser Nachtessen«, sagte Vater Eisbär und biss den Fisch in zwei Teile.
Nachdem sie gegessen hatten, war es Zeit zum Schlafen. »Lars, jetzt musst du einen
Schneehügel machen, um dich vor dem kalten Wind zu schützen«, sagte Vater Eisbär. Beide
schoben Schnee vor sich her, bis jeder seinen Schneehaufen errichtet hatte. Lars war stolz
auf seinen eigenen Schlafhügel und kuschelte sich zufrieden an den Schnee. So schliefen sie
bald ein.

When Lars woke up it was already light. He got quite a shock: there was water all around him! He was alone in the middle of the sea. Alone on a little island of ice with a small heap of snow. Where was his father? Lars felt desolate.

Als Lars aufwachte, war es schon Tag. Er erschrak: nichts als Wasser um ihn!
Er war ganz allein mitten im Meer! Allein auf einer kleinen Eisinsel mit dem kleinen Schneehaufen. Wo war sein Vater? Lars kam sich unendlich verlassen vor.

He felt unusually warm, too, and soon noticed that his ice floe was steadily shrinking. Then he saw a big barrel floating towards him. What a good thing it was that his father had shown him how to swim! He jumped bravely into the water and paddled over to the barrel. He pulled himself onto it and held on tight, because the wind was growing strong. Lars bobbed up and down on the waves.

Er spürte eine seltsame Wärme und merkte bald, dass seine Eisscholle immer kleiner wurde. Da entdeckte er ein großes Fass, das auf ihn zutrieb. Wie gut, dass sein Vater ihm gezeigt hatte, wie man schwimmt!
Mutig sprang er ins Wasser und paddelte zum Fass. Er zog sich hoch und hielt sich fest, denn ein heftiger Wind kam auf. Lars schaukelte mit den Wellen.

After the wind died down, Lars drifted across the sea for a long time.
The light grew ever brighter, and the air warmer. Suddenly he saw land
ahead of him, and it was green! Lars was amazed. This wasn't his white
home. Where could he be? He carefully slid off the barrel and splashed
through shallow water to the beach.

Als der Wind sich legte, trieb Lars lange auf dem Meer dahin. Es wurde
immer heller und wärmer. Plötzlich sah er Land vor sich. Grünes Land!
Lars staunte. Das war nicht sein weißes Zuhause! Wo war er nur
hingekommen? Vorsichtig rutschte Lars vom Fass und patschte durch
das seichte Wasser zum Ufer.

Lars's paws hurt when he walked across the hot sand. How he longed for snow and ice!
He turned back to cool his paws in the water. Just then an enormous animal burst out of
the water in front of him. "Booo!" it said. Lars ran away.
"Stop, stop! I was only playing!" called the big animal.

Lars taten die Pfoten weh, als er über den heißen Sand lief. Er sehnte sich nach Schnee
und Eis. Er kehrte um, weil er seine Pfoten im Wasser kühlen wollte.
Da tauchte vor ihm ein riesiges Tier auf. »Buuuuuh!«, machte es. Lars rannte weg.
»Halt, halt! Ich mache doch nur Spaß!«, rief das große Tier.

"I'm Henry the hippopotamus. Who are you? Why are you so white?"
Lars couldn't answer the last question. "Where I come from, everything is white!"
He wasn't afraid of Henry any more, and he told him about his long journey.
"I would really like to go home again," he said finally.

»Ich bin Hippo, das Flusspferd. Wer bist du? Warum bist du so weiß?«
Die letzte Frage konnte Lars nicht beantworten. »Da wo ich herkomme, ist einfach alles
weiß!« Er hatte nun keine Angst mehr vor Hippo und erzählte ihm von seiner weiten Reise.
»Ich würde gerne wieder nach Hause gehen«, sagte er am Ende.

Henry didn't need much time to think. "Marcus the eagle is the only one who can help you. He has travelled far and wide. He will know where you come from and how you can get back there," he explained.
"Come on, we have to cross the river and go up into the mountains."
"I can't – can't swim very well yet, you know," stuttered Lars.
"No problem!" laughed Henry. "Climb onto my back. I certainly won't sink."

Hippo überlegte nicht lange. »Der Einzige, der dir helfen kann, ist Drago, der Adler. Er ist weit in der Welt herumgekommen und wird schon wissen, woher du kommst und wie du wieder zurückkehren kannst«, erklärte er.
»Komm, wir müssen über den Fluss und dann in die Berge hinauf.«
»Ich kann – weißt du, ich kann noch nicht gut schwimmen«, stotterte Lars.
»Kein Problem!«, lachte Hippo. »Setz dich auf meinen Rücken, ich gehe bestimmt nicht unter!«

The trees and bushes, grass and flowers on the other bank amazed Lars. What a strange world! So many colours! He met a funny green animal that suddenly turned white. As white as Lars. "That's a chameleon," Henry explained. "It can change colour." Lars thought this was a very useful thing to be able to do.

Am anderen Ufer bestaunte Lars die Bäume und Sträucher, das Gras und die Blumen. Eine seltsame Welt! So viele Farben! Er begegnete einem komischen grünen Tier, das plötzlich weiß wurde. Weiß wie Lars. »Ein Chamäleon«, erklärte Hippo. »Es kann seine Farbe wechseln.« Lars fand das sehr praktisch.

Then they reached the mountains. It was not so hot here, and Lars felt more comfortable. Climbing wasn't easy for the hippo, however. Lars helped him, and showed him where to put his feet.

Dann kamen sie zu den Bergen. Hier war es nicht mehr so heiß und Lars fühlte sich viel wohler.
Für das Flusspferd war das Klettern jedoch nicht einfach. Lars half ihm und zeigte ihm die Stelle, wo es seine Füße hinsetzen konnte.

"That's enough for today!" sighed Henry, exhausted.
"Let's rest here. It's a beautiful spot!"
They looked far out across land and sea. Lars began to feel homesick.

»Das ist genug für heute!«, seufzte Hippo erschöpft.
»Lass uns hier ausruhen, es ist ein schöner Platz.«
Sie schauten weit über Land und Meer. Lars bekam Heimweh.

The next day they climbed higher. Henry had to keep stopping to catch his breath. He was keeping a constant look-out for Marcus.
"Here he comes!" he cried at last. Lars cowered before the big, unfamiliar bird.
"Good morning, Marcus," Henry said politely to the eagle as he landed. Then he explained briefly why he had brought Lars here.

Am nächsten Tag stiegen sie höher. Hippo musste immer wieder eine Pause machen und Atem schöpfen. Er hielt ständig nach Drago Ausschau.
»Dort kommt er!«, rief er endlich. Lars duckte sich vor dem großen, unbekannten Vogel.
»Guten Tag, Drago«, begrüßte Hippo freundlich den Adler, als dieser landete. Dann erklärte er kurz, warum er mit Lars hierher gekommen war.

Marcus looked at Lars. "Well, well, a polar bear in Africa! You are a long way from home, young fellow. But I know a whale that travels back and forth between here and the North Pole. He will take you with him. Wait for me and Samson in the cove tomorrow." "Thank you very, very much!" said Lars. Then they went back down the mountain.

Drago schaute Lars an. »Schaut, schaut, ein Eisbär in Afrika! Du bist weit weg von zu Hause, mein Kleiner. Aber ich kenne einen Wal, der reist zwischen hier und dem Nordpol hin und her. Er wird dich mitnehmen. Erwartet mich und Orka morgen in der Bucht.« »Vielen, vielen Dank!«, sagte Lars. Dann gingen sie wieder den Berg hinunter.

Lars ran ahead, fleet-footed because he was so happy to be going home. Henry plodded along behind with a heavy heart.
Early next morning they met Marcus and Samson in the cove. Henry was pleased that Lars could go home now, but he was very sad to be parted from his little friend. All he could say was, "Farewell".

Lars lief leichtfüßig voraus, die Freude auf die Heimreise trieb ihn an. Hippo stapfte hinterher. Sein Herz war schwer.
Früh am nächsten Morgen trafen sie Drago und Orka in der Bucht. Hippo freute sich, dass Lars nun nach Hause konnte. Aber die Trennung von seinem kleinen Freund fiel ihm schwer. »Leb wohl«, war alles, was er sagen konnte.

"Thank you so much for everything, dear Henry," cried Lars, once he was seated on the whale's back. Marcus flew along with them a little way.
Henry was left behind on his own. He stood alone on the beach for a long time after Lars was out of sight.

»Tausend Dank für alles, lieber Hippo!«, rief Lars, als er schon auf dem Wal saß.
Drago flog ein Stück weit mit.
Hippo blieb allein zurück. Er stand noch lange am Strand, als Lars schon nicht mehr zu sehen war.

"Your home must be somewhere around here," said the whale when they came to some big icebergs.
At that very moment Lars cried: "There's my father! Father! Father! Here I am!"
Father Polar Bear couldn't believe his eyes. There was Lars, on a whale's back!

»Hier ungefähr müsstest du zu Hause sein«, sagte Orka, als sie zu den großen Eisbergen kamen.
Im selben Augenblick rief Lars: »Dort ist mein Vater! Vater! Vater! Hier bin ich!«
Vater Eisbär traute seinen Augen nicht! Da war Lars, auf dem Rücken eines Wals!

Although Father Polar Bear was very tired from searching for Lars, he set off at once
to catch a beautiful big fish for Samson. The whale thanked him and then swam away.
"Now," said Father Polar Bear, "let's go home to your mother!"

Obwohl Vater Eisbär sehr müde war von der Suche nach Lars, machte er sich gleich daran,
einen schönen großen Fisch für Orka zu fangen. Der Wal dankte und schwamm gleich
wieder zurück. »Jetzt«, sagte Vater Eisbär, »gehen wir nach Hause zu deiner Mutter!«

Lars was allowed to sit on his father's back. He felt secure, holding on to his shaggy fur. Henry's back had been very slippery. They went back across the ice fields. Everything was white. Lars felt at ease. The last time they had passed this way, Father Polar Bear had told his son a lot of things. Now it was Lars who talked and talked. He talked about things his father had never seen.

"And no one there was white, no one at all?" asked Father Polar Bear in amazement.

"No, no one except a chameleon, but that doesn't count," said Lars, and he laughed.

Father Polar Bear didn't understand why Lars was laughing, but he was happy to have him back again.

Lars durfte auf Vaters Rücken sitzen. Er konnte sich im struppigen Fell gut festhalten. Bei Hippo war es sehr rutschig gewesen. Sie gingen über das große Eis zurück. Alles war weiß und kalt. Lars fühlte sich wohl. Als sie das letzte Mal diesen Weg gegangen waren, hatte Vater Eisbär seinem kleinen Sohn vieles erklärt. Nun war es Lars, der redete und redete. Er erzählte von Dingen, die sein Vater noch nie gesehen hatte.

»Und niemand ist dort weiß gewesen? Gar niemand?«, fragte Vater Eisbär erstaunt.

»Nein, niemand, außer einem Chamäleon. Aber das zählt nicht«, sagte Lars und lachte.

Vater Eisbär verstand nicht, worüber Lars lachte, aber er war glücklich, Lars wieder bei sich zu haben.